Commoner Marriage

By Antonino d'Este

Copyright, March 15th 2010

ISBN 978-0-557-38682-6

    A French-American Girl meets and consents to marry an Italian-American boy, all under the auspices of her employer, Georgio d'Este, a Prince of the House of Este

Dedicated to:

Vincent Temperino Jr, a friend of the family and best man at my nephew's wedding, and his lovely bride, Sylvette Bretey

Royal Crest of the House of Este

Books by Antonino d'Este

An American Duke
An American Sheik
I'll Tell You When the Night Comes
An American Duke in Italy
Duchinos and Duchessinas
Secrets of a Bounty Hunter
The Real Lucrezia Borgia
Clear the Bridge! Dive! Dive!
Kings without Crowns
The Reluctant Duke
I'll Think About It
The Diary of Gilda d'Este Colonna
Extended Family
The Money Rats
Commoner Marriage

Foreword

A young woman, Sylvette Bretey, travels to New York City looking for a position, and with the greatest of luck, stops at the offices of the d'Este Holding Company.

She is hired on the spot, and begins training under the watchful eye of Paula Imperioli, long-time secretary, first for Piero d'Este, Duke of Este, and then his son, Georgio.

After working in the office for seven months, her employer saw that Sylvette had special qualities, and decided to bring her under the protective umbrella of the powerful House of Este.

Sylvette did not fully understand the meaning of all this until she is introduced to Vincent Temperino Jr, a friend of the family, who falls in love with her and asks Georgio for her hand in marriage.

It is then that Sylvette realized that she is going to get the same treatment that a Princess of the House of Este is entitled to. She is awestruck, and grateful.

Chapter One

Paula Imperioli glanced up from her work and saw through the frosted glass the figure of a young woman standing outside of the entrance door to the office. This was not unusual, so she went back to her work and put the woman out of her mind.

Something made her look at the door again, and the figure was still there. This was odd. The printing on the glass said only, "Piero d'Este, Real Estate" and on the bottom the word "Enter"

She saw the knob turn slowly, timidly, and the young woman stepped in. Paula glanced at the woman, and with her practiced eye saw that she was new to New York City.

She intuitively knew that the woman was looking for employment, and was already thinking of how she would politely tell her that they were not hiring.

Sure enough, the woman asked if there were any openings for a beginner secretary, and Paula, indicating a chair, asked her to have a seat. There was a slight accent in the woman's voice and Paula deduced that it was of French origin.

While the accent had a sweet lilt to it, it didn't work in the woman's favor. Italians have a longstanding antipathy toward the French, going back to the days when the French kings habitually invaded and looted the Italian peninsular.

The d'Este family had a particular dislike of the French because one of the invading armies destroyed the tomb of Isabella d'Este, the first lady of the renaissance, and scattered her remains, which were never recovered.

However, Paula had a good heart, and even though help was not needed, decided to give the girl a far chance. "What is your name?"

"Sylvette Bretey"

"Have you had any experience at secretarial work?"

"Not very much! I'd be willing to start at a low salary."

"What brought you to this office?"

"I answered an ad for a job in another office in this building, but they had already hired someone, so I thought that as long as I was in the building, I'd ask at other offices."

Paula admired that. It showed good thinking, desire and ambition. She hired her as a temp, with the idea that she would give this young person some experience which would stand her in good stead when she went for a more permanent position.

"Oh, thank you! When can I start?"

"Right now! She took her to the filing room and had her sit behind a small table which was to serve as her desk. She quickly, yet patiently, showed Sylvette how the filing system worked, and then left her alone to figure things out.

Sylvette sat there for a few moments wondering what just happened, then started to study what had to be done. Once the idea settled into her mind that she had a job, her elation sent her floating up to cloud nine!

After two hours alone in the small room, she was glad to see Paula walk in with a smile on her face. She was in for a happy surprise.

"Here is your salary!" Paula said. "I'm paying your for the whole week!" She turned with an even bigger smile and left the room.

Sylvette opened the envelope and was amazed at the amount of money that was in it. In the face of such luck, her mind stopped working. What had she walked into?

When she came to her senses she said a little prayer of thanks to the Lord, and then remembered that she had to earn her money, and went back to the files.

She soon learned that her job was going to expand. She was to stop off at a store for Danish and such, and make the coffee each morning.

One morning she was asked to bring a breakfast tray to the boss in the inner sanctum.

Georgio d'Este looked up as she entered and asked, "Who are you?"

Flustered at standing before the big boss, she stammered, "I'm Sylvette, the new girl."

"Oh!" After a pause he said, "I didn't know we had a new girl. All right, put the tray here, and thank you."

She practically ran out of the room and Paula was giggling at her discomfort. "He's really something, isn't he Sylvette?"

The "new girl" couldn't say a word. Paula giggled again as Sylvette tip-toed back into her little room.

After an hour, she came out again and asked, "How come he didn't know I was hired?"

"I don't bother him with such details. He keeps his mind on the big picture, and I'm free to run this office."

"What is the big picture? I mean, what do you do here?"

"Sylvette, it's right there on the door! We're in the real estate business."

"Paula, when I looked into his eyes I was daunted at the ferocious look in them. Is he a very cold man?"

"Not at all! He's a member of a very powerful family and is aware of that power."

"You don't mean that he's connected, do you? I don't mean to be impolite, but is there anything illegal going on?"

"Of course not, you silly girl! You've been working on the files, so you can see what's going on. It's all real estate, and certain holdings."

"What are those holdings? I can't make that out."

The d'Este family acts like a private bank for the Italian community. People who want to save their money here simply make a deposit, and we open an account for them. For that they receive interest, and the money is used to buy income producing commercial property."

"Are these accounts insured?"

"The word of the family is all the insurance the depositors need."

"Oh my! This is quite a family, isn't it?"

Paula laughed. "You don't know what you've gotten yourself into!"

Sylvette laughed too, and then repeated, "Oh my!"

She was to spend a lot of her time shopping for office supplies, and ordering and bringing lunches to the office, and running other errands, such as going to the post office, and spelling Paula at the main desk when the secretary took her break.

One thing Sylvette had to learn quickly. She had to know who Il Senor Georgio wanted on the phone, or who came to see him in his office.

This was not so simple a matter. Some people were dressed to the nines, and others looked scruffy.

The last thing she wanted to do was to make the mistake of letting someone in who was not authorized. She felt instinctively that this could lead to bad situations.

"Don't let that worry you too much." Paula said. "When in doubt, just announce the visitor and let the boss make the decision. It's the same with incoming phone calls."

Sylvette was getting used to the work and becoming quite efficient, but she was ever aware that she was hired on a temporary basis, so she didn't take anything for granted.

She said, "I wish I was an Italian, so that I could feel more secure in my job." But Paula only laughed and didn't say anything. That was not so re-assuring.

Then one day, after many months, Senor Georgio called Paula into his office and said, "The new girl, Sylvette, is solid and trustworthy. Bring her under the family umbrella."

When Paula came out of the office, she went to Sylvette and said, "My dear girl, you have just been made permanent!"

"Oh, how wonderful! I must call my parents and tell them I have a permanent job with a very nice firm. They'll be happy to know that I'm not in an insecure position."

"Before you call them, let's go in and thank the boss."

When they went into the inner sanctum and were seated, Senor Georgio pored out a small glass of blackberry brandy and toasted a blushing Sylvette with the words, "Welcome into the extended family."

He then gave her a cautionary speech. "Do not talk about anything that goes on here to anyone, not even your family or friends. Just say you're a secretary, and let it go at that. Within this family, trust is paramount. You mustn't slip up. Mum's the word."

Sylvette nodded, but didn't understand it all. "Why such secrecy?" she wondered.

Senor Giorgio cleared that up right away, as if reading her mind. "There isn't anything about the business with the public that we want to hide.

It's the privacy of the family that we are extremely careful to keep from outsiders. You will never see anything written or said about us in the media. We don't want to be bothered by anyone."

She was to learn in time how serious the family was about avoiding publicity. She was also to learn that their interest extended to five countries, and went far beyond New York City.

What she never quite realized was how the family kept its privacy, and the lessons learned by anyone who tried to pry.

He went on. "Sylvette, if anyone wants to pump you for information, report that directly to me. Is that clear?"

"Yes sir. I know what I have to do, and I feel it is in my own interests to obey you completely."

"Very good! I'm proud of you. Paula, when John Lombardi arrives, please send him in." The meeting was over.

Chapter Two

John Lombardi walked in and with just a cursory nod to Paula, went directly into the inner office. He dropped into a chair and asked, "Georgio, do you have something for me?"

"Yes, John. You're renovating one of the apartments in our building on East 58th Street, right?"

"Yes, we should be finished there in about a week."

"Fine! The maintenance man has his apartment on the first floor, and his work room is also on that floor. I want his work space to be moved into the basement next to the laundry room, and that first floor space converted into a small apartment for a single girl."

"Somebody special?"

"I had an agent look into the place where the new assistant secretary is living, and it's a hovel, so I want her moved to a safer building. She'll be closer by, and can walk to work when the weather permits. John, do a good job, but work quickly. I don't want Sylvette staying in that rat's nest for too long. I may even ask Paula to take her in for a while."

"A bad place, huh?"

"The very worst! How do these slumlords get away with what they do? They should be hung!"

"Yeah! Well, the young women have to be blamed, too. They come to New York cold turkey, and expect to make it big. All too soon they discover that the city is a meat grinder for those who do not know how to live here. I'll get right on the new project."

"Make sure it has everything for her comfort and security. Hire a decorator, too. When it's almost ready, we'll have Sylvette look at it and choose her colors."

"She's a lucky girl, Georgio."

"She deserves it."

When John said he's get right on it, he wasn't kidding. Realizing the need for haste, he soon had a swarm of workers preparing the new place, and the office started receiving complaints from the residents about the noise and the fuss.

Paula handled all the complaints and smoothed the ruffled feathers of the people who had to put up with it, and all the while, Sylvette was oblivious to the fact that it was all for her that this was going on. The boss loved to surprise people.

It became obvious to Paula that Il Senor Georgio was "adopting" the petite "Frenchie" as another daughter. She, having gotten used to having Sylvette around, understood why he was so protective. She was well bred, but naïve and vulnerable.

The renovation took longer than both Senor Georgio and John Lombardi liked, but that's because the space needed everything. There were only a few workbenches, wood horses and lot of tools and equipment for the maintenance man's use, and a huge slop silk.

First everything had to be moved to the basement, the sink taken out, then the plumbing and wiring for the kitchenette and a totally new bathroom had to be installed.

The woodwork took extra time too, but what excellent work the Temperino men were doing! That they were available for this project was a testimony to the respect they had for the d'Este family.

And so it went, but the day came when Senor Georgio, pretending to take Sylvette to lunch, took her instead to her new apartment. There were still workers around, but waiting for them was the interior decorator, who surprised Sylvette by asking her want colors she wanted on the walls and for the rug.

Learning that this was HER new apartment caused Sylvette to burst into tears. Her eyes were so filled that it took a while before she could even see the color cards and samples the decorator was displaying.

Senor Georgio consoled her while a grinning John Lombardi stood by. The Temperino men were preoccupied with their own work and didn't notice the slip of a girl crying her eyes out.

At this time Sylvette did not know about the family except that they had power. She had yet to learn that they were old royalty as well.

The decorator had to coax and coach Sylvette until the colors were chosen, and then informed her that in a few days someone will take her shopping for the furniture.

Sylvette felt a little dizzy by this grand surprise, and when she was taken to lunch by Senor Georgio and John Lombardi, she couldn't decide what to order.

John decided for her. He ordered a delicious anti-pasta, then veal cutlets and a side of angel hair pasta with salsa al pomadoro, some creamed spinach.

Then the obligatory glass of Vino di Tavola was served, which Sylvette, being of French extraction, handled easily. Finally, all this was followed by the sweets, and a rather small cup of Cappuccino.

The wine helped Sylvette find her voice, and she thanked the men for everything. When Senor Georgio told her she had become like a daughter to him, her eyes began to well up again.

John made a joke, saying, "Don't be so sure this is a privilege. You'd better talk to one of his daughters first." They all laughed, and that broke the tension.

Back at the office Sylvette happily told Paula the exciting news, and Paula tried to look surprised and happy for her. Then Sylvette called her parents and told of the new apartment her boss was setting up for her, but instead of a happy reaction, the feathers hit the fan

Her mother fairly screamed into the phone, "Are you going to be a kept woman? You'd better come home immediately!"

Paula, seeing the look on the girl's face, took the phone, and with the greatest patience, told her parents that there was absolutely nothing amiss, and that she would be happy to pay their air fares to New York so that they can meet Senor Georgio and see the true situation for themselves.

This mollified them temporarily, but Paula wisely prepared a follow-up letter to them from the boss himself, assuring them that all that was being done was for Sylvette's protection and comfort, and no more than that.

Sylvette gave the letter time to reach her parents, then called them again to reassure them that she is a good girl and will retain her virtue at all times. She promised to send them photographs of the building and the interior of her apartment. Apparently they finally relaxed, because no more was heard about the issue.

One morning she stopped at the store for breakfast buns, came in and made the coffee and sat with Paula while they ate. The door opened and in walked a very finely dressed woman. She was not only beautiful, but very stately in her manner.

Paula stood up and came to attention, and Sylvette, copying her, did the same. Paula said, "Good morning, Countess." And Sylvette, nonplussed, followed suit, by saying timidly, "Good morning, Ma'am"

The woman said, "Good morning! Good morning! This must be my charge for the day?"

"Yes, this is Sylvette."

"Fine!" she said as she appraised the girl, and then said, "I'll see my brother-in-law Georgio for a few minutes, and then we'll go shopping!" She breezed into the inner office, leaving a pleasant, smell of expensive perfume in the air.

"Shopping?"

"Yes," Paula said, smiling. "Today you pick out your furniture."

"But who is THAT?"

"That is the Duke's sister, Francesca."

"I don't understand. Why did you call her Countess?"

"Because that's what she is!

"Is she Royalty?"

"The whole family is. Our boss holds the title of Count."

"Oh Lord! I can't go shopping with her! How do I act? What should I do? Paula, this is scaring me!"

"Relax! I'll go along with you, although I don't see what you're worried about. Francesca is one of the kindest persons ever, and she'll treat you like a queen."

Paula looked in on Senor Georgio and excused herself. "I'll be back in a couple of hours."

At the first furniture store they went to the decorator was waiting for them. She had the floor plan and all the measurements of the new apartment, and as they looked at pieces, they measured to see what would fit and if it pleased Sylvette.

She knew she was out-classed , so she said that she would be pleased with anything they chose for her. Paula gave her a nod and a smile.

It was clear that Francesca and the decorator knew what they were doing. Since the apartment was so small, they chose a nice adjustable single bed which would serve as both a bed and a lounge.

A bedside table and a lamp were ordered, and a dinette set with two leatherette chairs on wheels. Each piece they bought was marked on the diagram and soon, except for all the trimmings, they were essentially done.

Sylvette was very happy with the vanity and its mirrors. The ladies knew that this particular piece would get a lot of use. What lady of fashion could live without a complete vanity?

The ladies insisted that Sylvette choose her own dishes, pots, towels, flatware and other incidentals. Since they were shopping in the finest stores, she could not possible buy junk.

They were done, and except for the decorator, the group was back at the office in no time. When Senor Georgio stepped out of the office, Sylvette ran up to him as an excited girl would run to her father, and hugged him tightly. There were smiles all around, and the Senor said, "I think it's dinner time!"

Chapter Three

"Mister Imperioli, I want to thank you and Paula for giving me such a nice room in your apartment, and treating me like one of the family. Everyone has been so kind to me ever since I walked into the Holding Company office. My life has been like a fairy tale ever since."

"Sylvette, you ARE one of the family, now, and please call me Santo. You're welcome to stay here as long as you like"

"I hope I'm not in the way! It will only be for a short time."

"Sylvette, we enjoy having you stay with us. I have only one concern when you move into your own apartment. Before you came to New York you lived with your parents, and you had two roommates in your apartment here. In your new apartment you're going to be alone for the first time. Can you handle that?"

"I don't know. Have you ever lived alone Paula?"

"No. I was living with my family when Santo came into my life. We were married not long after we met."

"Oh, please tell me how you met!"

Santo said, "She threw a lasso around me and tied me up!"

"I did not! Don't go making up stories! No, Santo was my brother's friend, and one day he came to dinner. I liked him immediately and later that night I walked him to the door and said, 'Well, are you coming back, or what?'

He said, "Do you want me to?" and I said "yes!"'"

"That's when she tied me up!"

"Oh, stop it! When he did come back he had a bouquet of flowers, and not long after that we were engaged."

"That's so romantic! I hope I can meet a nice man soon."

Santo looked at her with an appreciative eye and said, "You will, my dear, you will!"

"Paula said, "Down, boy! Don't get frisky!" To Sylvette she said, "He's right, though. You will not have trouble attracting the young men, but you're in New York City now, and finding a good man can be a serious problem. We'll ask Senor Georgio to keep an eye out for one."

"We can't do that! I feel embarrassed already just at the thought of asking him that."

Santo said, "Sylvette, listen to Paula. The city is crawling with guys that seem nice at the beginning, but can turn out to be monsters in one form or another. We'll all keep an eye out for a real man. We can make a game of it."

"Santo, this is not a game. It's a very serious matter!" Paula was in earnest.

"OK, how about your brother Joe?"

"He's keeping company, Santo! Try to stay with the times, will you?"

This bantering went on for a while, but soon it was bed time and work the next day. In the morning, the two women stopped off for some breakfast goodies for the office, and after Sylvette made the coffee, she said, "You and

Santo get along so well. You seem so content and comfortable with each other that I feel a pinch of jealousy."

"Remember what was said last night. There are real creeps running around, so don't be hasty in you desire to be with a man. Wait! You'll be glad you did."

"Paula, may I confess something deeply personal? I hope you don't mind."

"Not at all! Go ahead."

"There are times when I want a man to touch me. The feeling gets so strong that I want to run into the street and jump on the first man I meet. I've kept it under control up to now, but I fear that one of these days I'm going to lose my cool. My vulva is talking to me! Am I sick?"

"You're very normal. You've matured, and this is God's way of telling you to procreate. Be patient. You're pretty, and it won't be long before someone will notice you. It also won't be long before we're going to have to start weeding them out!" They laughed, and it was time to go to work.

Paula brought the breakfast tray into the boss's office, and he asked what the hilarity was all about. Paula, sotto voce, told him what the topic of discussion was, and he agreed that a good man had to be found soon. Young women, sensible in every way, will step into hell when their hormones are raising a fuss.

"We must keep her busy. Take her shopping for all the necessities that keep a home running. Music rolls. kitchen towels, throw rugs, pillows and slips, anything like that."

"Music rolls?"

"Yes, toilet paper!"

Paula laughed. "I never heard them called THAT before, but it sort of makes sense, doesn't it?"

"You never heard it? That's been around for ages. When you're in your own place, make a list with her about all the things you have that she should buy at the store. That way she won't forget anything. By the way, tell her not to go out at night. That building is in a nice neighborhood, but one never knows."

"All your buildings are in nice neighborhoods, senor, except perhaps the lofts your father bought and renovated in Greenwich Village."

"They're all right, if you consider the people who want to rent them. They like to think of themselves as artists. What a laugh!"

That night Santo, Paula and Sylvette had a lot of fun making up the shopping list for the new apartment. Santo said, "If you call toilet paper music rolls, then let's give names to other products."

They couldn't come up with anything until Santo said, "Aquarta milk, aloafa bread!"

"Now you're getting silly!" Paula said.

"Well, YOU try!"

"People call beans gas pills" Sylvette said.

"My brother calls tea panther piss."

"Don't be obscene, Santo!"

And so it went, until they had made a list that was going to cost a bundle. "We don't have to buy everything at once. Nobody does that", Paula said.

They went to their beds satisfied that they thought of everything. Moving day was getting closer, and maybe they should start moving the groceries in now. No, not while there were still workmen there. There would be plenty of time for such trivia.

With the idea of keeping Sylvette distracted, Senor Georgio gave her an extra assignment. Three days a week she was to leave work early and report to the family communications center which was located in the New York apartment of Duke Antonino III Vincenti, known as Vince.

"He is Georgio's nephew, and the one who was chosen to succeed the Senior Duke Antonino II, now retired to Saint Petersburg, Florida."

She added that Vince maintains his apartment in the city for his use when he comes to America, and his desk is used to shuttle messages from one branch of the family to the others.

"This desk was being manned by an old friend and co-conspirator Marco Astuzia, who worked with Vince on several 'projects' in the past. We don't refer to those projects as 'raids' anymore."

Now Sylvette was to learn the ropes and spell Marco at the desk on certain evenings so that he can get a break now and then.

At first sight, Sylvette thought she found the man of her dreams, but sadly for her, the handsome Marco was married, and his playful days were long over.

She was to discover, however, that he liked to play practical jokes, and was told to examine carefully everything he says and does.

For the first week Marco stayed with her, showing her every facet of the job, but there were a few things he didn't go into. One was that the Duke in Italy was carrying on a private chat with a woman he "met" on "My Space" on the web.

They had never met or spoke on the phone, confining their chat to e-mail messages only. They were having fun, and sometimes the chats got a little raunchy, but all for laughs. Finally Marco told her that when a message came in for "Idalee", she was to monitor it and send it on.

What Marco did not say was that Sylvette should always maintain aloofness in transferring messages. She was never to get into the chat herself, although he confessed later that he himself yielded to the temptation.

She discovered that Idalee called the Duke "Tony" which was odd because very few people did that. They were having so much fun in their chats that she began making comments herself.

She and Idalee started chatting too, and soon, the young Sylvette was seeking advice from the mature woman in Walla Walla, Washington. She complained about the lack of a man in her life, and other female issues.

Idalee was a kind and understanding person that Sylvette opened her heart to her, and some of their chats got quite personal. It seems that Idalee understood that she was chatting with, and guiding a naïve girl with very little real life experience.

After a time, Sylvette got some good advice, and Idalee got a good insight into the temper of the members of the House of Este. Sylvette forgot the admonition of Georgio about saying too much to strangers. However, it would be some time before this mild transgression was discovered.

Meanwhile, there was no real harm being done, since, fortunately, Idalee was a woman of the highest discretion. The two women soon regarded themselves as kindred spirits.

Idalee was steeped in the arts, so when she learned that Sylvette was taking piano lessons, she was supportive and even gave her some hints on practicing and getting feeling into the music.

Sylvette was fascinated by the mere fact that she was chatting with a ballet dancer and teacher. The disparate women found that their personalities dovetailed nicely.

Then events started taking a new turn. Marco went off to Atlanta, Georgia, to engage in a dangerous adventure. Some men got together to form a gang of entrepreneurs to raid the drug cartels operating in that area.

The men were not leaders and the whole project was taking a bad turn when Marco asked Vince to come to Atlanta and take over leadership. This story is told completely in the author's book, "The Money Rats" and this narrative concerns itself with the story of Sylvette Bretey.

Once Vince agreed to take part in the operation, Sylvette had to put in more time at the communication desk because of all the messages that were flying back and fourth. This took her out of the office and Paula hired another acolyte to replace her.

Sylvette had already moved into her new apartment, but was not spending much time there. She was living in Vince's apartment most of the time, and getting a lot of training on the computer.

Vince played the piano, and there was a beautiful baby grand in his apartment. Sylvette sat at the piano to toy around, but soon decided that she wanted to learn how to play it.

Senor Georgio got her a teacher, and it developed that Sylvette was a natural. She picked it up so fast that even the teacher was amazed.

She told Senor Georgio, "I've had precocious students before, but this girl is a truly fast learner. I never saw anyone so eager to advance.

Now that she had music, the thoughts of romance dimmed a bit, but occasionally her vulva "spoke" to her again, and she daydreamed of her knight in shining armor. Like so many dreamy girls, the knight she imagined was never going to be found, simply because he didn't exist!

+

Chapter Four

The months went by with the family concerned over the safety of the Duke Vince and his friends in Atlanta. They were eager for details, but the men had to be circumspect, and so the family only got the sketchiest of information.

There was no escaping the fact that the men were in terrible danger, but they were seasoned raiders, most of them, so if anyone could pull these raids off, they were the ones to do it.

After many weeks the Duchess Gilda in Italy was despairing for the safety of her husband. She was young, and could not understand why he would leave her, an expectant mother, to go off on such an adventure.

She kept asking anyone who would listen if this mission was worth the risk.

She would never know how many millions of dollars were involved, and probably would not have cared. All she wanted was to have her husband at home.

It takes a long time for women to begin understanding men. The opposite is also true.

Who said, "Ours is not to reason why, ours is not to give reply, ours is but to do or die." I think that had something to do with the charge of the light brigade.

Anyway, some people have to charge, and others have to wait. The family started to feel better when they began to get news of successes, and that the business was getting close to completion.

When the first shipment of money came to the Holding Company, the family was flabbergasted! Nobody dreamed that this project was going to be that lucrative, and that was only part of it.

Even so, everyone worried. Things can go wrong even with the most experienced of men.

The pressure began to affect Sylvette in a strange way. She began to be overly worried about Marco. She had warm feelings for him, and now that it began to look like the boys were working in a very dangerous situation, she kept calling Paula and Santo for consolation.

She was told by both of them that the men in Atlanta were real professionals and that if anyone was in trouble it was the people who are running the drug cartels.

Santo was very emphatic about that point, but was only trying to soothe Sylvette's anxiety. He had no idea what the real situation was in Atlanta.

The newspapers, radio or television were no help at all, and that puzzled the people who were trying to get up-to-date information.

The reason was simple. The entrepreneurs were not saying anything, and the cartel people didn't know who was hitting them, and it certainly was in own their interest not to get the police or anyone else involved.

The "war" went on quietly, and the cartels began blaming each other for their losses and misfortune. The main Atlanta cartel had been weakened by attrition, and when Vince's gang hit the headquarters itself and killed two of the people in the house, the drug dealers were shaken.

The raiders then calmly loaded several million dollars into a waiting car, and faded into the night.

The big bosses in Mexico were so furious that they had their own man-in-charge executed.

Collections continued to be sent to the main house, however. so Vince's men hit it again. How stupid can these Hispanics be?

That was the last straw for the Hispanics. They moved out of Atlanta, and the men who "relieved" them of all that money quietly left for home.

The family was relieved when the project was finally over. Most of the money went to the coffers of the Holding company as investments in the accounts of the individuals involved, and Duke Vince, after a short stay to see that everything was properly organized, went home to his young Gilda.

Sylvette was happy to meet the junior Duke, and so relieved to see Marco again, so much so that she came close to offering him her favors.

She was saved from her own folly when she was recalled to the office to work on the new accounts.

She briefly met Marco's wife Cathy when she came to the apartment to bring him his lunch. When Sylvette saw how beautiful Cathy was, she felt her own education become more complete. Marco was not going to play with HER!

She talked to Paula and told of her near mistake, and Paula assured her once again that a nice man was on the way, and she just had to wait.

Sylvette wondered how her man would ever find her while she worked at the communication desk or in the file room at the office. A short time after that, she was invited to have Sunday dinner with Georgio and the family

Also invited were Mister Vincent Temperino Senior, and his son. The younger Vincent was seated directly opposite Sylvette so that they could look directly at each other.

Young Vincent was a tall, strong man, and Sylvette quite petite. It looked like a miss-match for certain. Sylvette furtively studied him, but he seemed oblivious of her presence.

He wasn't really. She was pretty, that he saw, but he was girl-shy and was unable to make a sign that he liked her. Neither one of them were told that this was a bit of match-making by senor Georgio and Vincent's father.

The dinner ended with apparently no results, so the idea was given up. Young Vincent didn't give up, though, and thought long and hard about how he could get closer the French girl.

He would wait forever, if he didn't make his wishes known. Sylvette could not encourage him. She was not to see him for months on end.

He thought he would hang out in front of her building to "accidentally" bump into her, but which building? She spent more time in Vince's apartment than she did in her own, going there to play the piano, and being close to Marco. It was a confusing time all around for the young people.

She not only enjoyed doing some work at the communications desk, but she was held there by the piano and her studies and the exciting presence of the Italian. There was no way that she could get a piano in her own apartment. Even a small electronic keyboard would barely fit on the dinette table.

Besides, no electronic piano would have the rich, throaty sound of the baby grand. She was playing medium level classical pieces as though she had been practicing for years. Thoughts of the poor, shy Vincent took second place at this time.

Cathy was also 'visiting' more often. There was no reason to be suspicious. Marco loved her and would not stray, but women have to leave their 'markings' on their 'territory', don't they?

One day, after work at the office, Senor Georgio said he would take Sylvette home. "I want to take a look at the new apartment now that it's finished. Paula, will you come with us? Ask Al, the maintenance-manager to meet us."

Al was waiting when they got there and Sylvette opened the door and they went in. Senor Georgio said, I didn't know it was so small! We'll never get a keyboard in here!"

Al said, "May I remind you, Sir, that there's an apartment upstairs that has been renovated and is empty."

"I know, Al, but we have to have the rental for that space. It goes for three thousand two hundred dollars a month."

Sylvette said, "Oh, my!" and Paula laughed. She asked, "What did you think New York apartments go for?"

Sylvette whispered, "What would mine cost?"

"You have nothing to worry about there, my dear."

Al chimed in. "Your very lucky, Sylvette."

Senor Georgio snapped at him. "You will call her Miss Bretey, Al! There's no excuse for such familiarity!"

"Yes, Sir! No offense intended."

This was the only building owned by the d'Este Holding Company that had a custodian-manager. Some of the buildings had managers, and the custodial work was done by an outside contractor. Paula would call them when they were needed.

The converted lofts in the Greenwich Village area didn't have any services. If something broke then a man was sent to repair it, but the people there were responsible for their own cleaning. If they didn't clean, then they lived in their own mess.

Those tenants were promised that if they allowed there spaces to get too messy, they would be tossed out into the street, and they believed it, because they saw it happen.

Things stayed the way they were for Sylvette, for the time being. It was expected that she would marry, so the small apartment would do for a while.

The shy young Vincent buried himself in his work and tried to forget the French girl. Then one day, on the job with his father, he mentioned that she was nice, and the father's ears perked up.

"Are you interested, son?"

"I'm not sure, but I remember her well. Didn't you think she was pretty?"

"Yes indeed, and well mannered, too! I'm sure you'll be meeting her again."

"Do you think so? Where will I meet her?"

"That I don't know, but things have a way of coming around again. I'll bet dollars to donuts that you'll meet her again."

Of course he will. Now that he mentioned her, Vincent Senior will be talking to Senor Georgio again. The first chance he got he called his wife and said, "Hot dog! Vinny is thinking about the French Girl."

He heard his wife say, "Ingraziam' a Dio!"

The wheels started turning, slowly at first, then they began to take a momentum of their own. Still, time went by before any first steps were made by the family.

Meanwhile the two romantically fated kids were sublimely ignorant of the "plots" involving them. More and more people got in on the "secret" and suggestions were flying all over the place.

Finally Sylvette was called into Senor Georgio's office and told to practice a few pieces on the piano so that she can give the family a recital at the family home.

"Oh my! When?"

"In about a month's time. I want to hear you play. After all, I want my money's worth for all the music lessons," and he laughed.

"Oh, Sir, La Senora is a concert pianist. I'm already quivering in my boots."

"Nonsense! She'll understand, and besides, if she does offer any criticism, it will be positive. She likes you a lot, you know!"

"I didn't know, but that helps, a little!"

Well, you go ahead and practice, three pieces will be enough, and I'm sure you know many more than that. It's all right if you choose easy ones. Just be sure of your technique and expression."

"Ill try, Sir, and thank you."

She ran out to Paula in a panic and told her what had just happened. Paula acted both surprised and pleased, but actually she was in on it all along. Everybody loves match-making, and Paula was no exception.

Chapter Five

Now Sylvette practically lived at the piano whenever she had a spare minute, but she would never attain the confidence she so desperately wanted. She stuck to Paula like glue looking for encouragement, and even got on the computer to tell of her plight to the lady Idalee.

That lady knew plenty about what Sylvette was going through and told her that everyone gets nervous, but that they do well when the test came. That advice made her feel better, because she was sure she knew the work. She just had to conquer her nervousness.

Marco and Cathy were prevailed upon to listen to her play. She asked them to comment on her technique and her musical expression, but they were not musicians, and could only say they liked the way she played.

Still, that was something, so she decided that, come what may, she would go with what she had. Now, if only she could get a good night's sleep!

As the day approached, she felt that her nerves were getting raw. As she practiced, there was a visitor at the door. To everyone's surprise, it was Francesca, Duke Vince's sister.

"Please keep playing, Sylvette! I like what you're doing."

To her own surprise, Sylvette continued as smoothly as if she were playing alone, and with that request her spirits began to soar. When she had completed her three pieces, Francesca applauded and Marco and Cathy joined in.

"She asked sheepishly, "Do you think I'm ready for my first recital?"

Francesca said, "You mean your SECOND recital. You just played your first one."

"That's right! I did!"

This called for some sort of celebration, and Francesca took the three of them out to dinner. Sylvette now came to believe how wonderful a person Francesca truly was. The royal lady had made a friend for life.

They imbibed in a second glass of wine, and everyone began to get a little mellow. When they got back to the apartment, Sylvette was asked to play again, which she did with flair and relish.

Francesca said, "Do that for the family, and you'll be a sensation." Everybody laughed, and they spent a good night chatting and telling humorous stories.

Francesca told some stories about the Duke Vince, which he would have preferred no one knew about. But it was all in fun, and he would have laughed at the way she told them.

There was no way of stopping the clock, and soon the day came for the recital at the home of the d'Estes. Sylvette was having a case of nerves again as she walked into the building.

This building was a rarity in New York City, a building wholly occupied by one family. One walked into a large foyer and saw another rarity, an elevator.

She never saw the makeup of the rooms on the first floor. On her last visit, the dining room was on the second floor and the music room on the third.

Some refreshment were served, and it was time for Sylvette to step up to the piano. This one was a concert grand, and she felt awed by it, but at least she knew it was played exactly the same way, so she began her short program.

She felt a little tension when she started, but soon the piano itself seem to cooperate, and she did the music justice. There was a round of applause, and when she made her bows, she noticed that the younger Vincent Temperino was in attendance.

Senor Georgio brought her a bouquet of flowers, and Senora Anitra gave her a small present. It was a white box tied with purple ribbon.

"May I open it, Senora?" Sylvette asked

She smiled and said, "I insist that you do."

Sylvette opened it very carefully, so much so that someone said, "Hurry up!" and everyone laughed.

She saw a purple case inside, and in that was a diamond bracelet. The people saw that

Sylvette was about to cry when Senora Anitra said, "It's my turn to entertain.

Senor Georgio got up too, and while she played a few pieces from the various operas, he sang. They were excellent.

Lunch was announced, and Sylvette saw that she was once again seated directly across from Vincent. This time he opened his mouth. He complimented her on her playing and, blushing, said he would like to hear more in the future.

There were broad smiles around the table as the people were pleased with their conspiracy. The kids would certainly meet again, but there was one more step to be taken. Vincent had to propose.

That was going to take time and more maneuvering. However, all the elements of success were indicated, and the group was actively congratulating each other with their eyes.

Vincent will become the independent individual his parents were hoping to see, and Sylvette will be saved from her own passionate nature.

But again, these things take time. The kids have to grow into the idea, and who knows how their ideas will run in the coming months and years.

At least the first step was in the right direction, in that they looked at each other and were speaking. Now it will be up to the hormones to kick in, and the pheromones to do their work.

Some of the conspirators wanted to start planning the wedding. All that got is laughs and some mild derision. Still, we never know how horny the principles really are.

"They may elope!" Someone suggested.

"No, that would be disrespectful and insulting. They might be told that, just incase they get the idea."

"Don't worry about that! If they do elope, we'll just put them through the wedding anyway. No one is going to cheat ME out of a big party!" Paula said. That brought more laughs and a lot of agreement.

When lunch was about over, Senora Anitra suggested that Paula and Santo take a turn around the garden and see the new arrangements.

Then, as an "afterthought", suggested they take Sylvette and Vincent with them and show them around.

This gave Santo a few ideas. As the two couples walked around the winding path, Santo saw a small bench almost hidden away under a trellis. He said to his wife, "Sit here! This is the kissing bench."

Paula quickly caught on and they kissed once, then twice, and then got up and continued walking, but Santo called back, saying, "Don't pass the kissing bench!"

The slow-witted Vincent was about to walk passed it when Sylvette insisted that they sit down. Vincent protested, saying that the others were moving ahead, but she was going to have a few kisses too, so she pushed him down, sat on him and kissed him soundly.

He started kissing her back, and when she got up to continue the walk, he was too ashamed to stand up. Blushing and perspiring, he tried to hide the rammer that was trying to jump out of his pants.

For her part, Sylvette felt a strong desire to lift her dress and sit on it. Later, when she told this story to Cathy, she relayed it to Marco, and the practical joker got an idea that was to play out later on with interesting consequences that changed the course of the family history.

Chapter Six

Sylvette didn't practice her piano lessons for a few days, needing a rest from all the excitement of the recital, the lunch and the "kissing bench." Besides, she had to catch up on her office work, and needed some alone time in her apartment to think about what transpired, and how it all would effect her future.

As much as she wanted a lover, she had some reservations about Vincent. She thought she should look for someone a little closer to her age, for one thing, and for another, she was not too thrilled about his shyness.

She didn't feel she had to push a man into kissing her, or even feeling her under her dress. She was more than ready for that kind of thrill, and certainly any other man given that kind of invitation would have given her vulva a good touch up.

She ran the day over and over in her mind. She was happy that she played well for the family, and she was elated whenever she looked at her diamond bracelet, but she was unsure about Vincent.

The flowers she was given now displayed their beauty in a nice vase in the center of her dinette table, and she could smell their perfume all over the small apartment.

So why should she feel this slight discontent? She did feel some shame at not being totally happy with the late events. Was she being disloyal to Senor and Senora d'Este? Was she an ingrate?

The more she turned things over in her mind, the further she got from the answers she sought. She would have to talk to someone. It can't be Paula. She was too close to the family, and totally loyal to them.

Why not Marco and Cathy? She had her phone in the apartment now, so she sat on the bed and reached for it. She called the communications desk and Marco answered.

"Marco, I'd like to come over for my piano practice, but I would also like to talk to Cathy. Can she be there tomorrow?"

"Of course, Sylvette! Is anything wrong?"

"No really. I'm just a bit muddled."

"I understand! That was a big day for you, wasn't it?"

"It sure was! I'm living in the middle of a dream, and trying to get back down to earth."

"Don't hurry! A lot of women your age would love to be living in your dream. Besides, you really are down to earth. You just have to wake up to that."

"You may be right! I hope Cathy can help me shake the fog out of my brain. I can't think this thing through!"

"Good luck with that! My Cathy has been in her own fog ever since I met her. Even before that!" She heard him laugh, and then he said, "I have an incoming! See you tomorrow!" and he hung up.

Then Sylvette thought, "Idalee would be a good person to talk to. Why didn't I think of that before?" She'd have to wait until she had the chance to e-mail her, thought. That was the only way to reach her.

Then she remembered Senor Georgio's proscription and thought, "I wonder how much I can safely say? Well, if it's just personal stuff, it should be all right."

She went to bed, but the big problems that were of her own making were keeping her awake until the wee hours. Actually the only issue she had was simply this: Should she continue to see Vincent? He said he would call her. Should she see him again?

She was bleary eyed and sluggish at work but Paula didn't say anything. She understood, and had to wait for Sylvette to open that conversation. At the end of the day, Sylvette went straight to Vince's apartment.

Cathy had some wine and cheese ready and the two women sat down at the table. Marco was at the desk, so he couldn't overhear the conversation. He didn't have to. He knew what was on Sylvette's mind, and he also knew that Cathy was not going to be a lot of help.

Sometimes women can come to terms with their issues just by talking about them. That's what was going to happen here. Marco couldn't resist the temptation of messaging His grace, Duke Vince, and giving him the lowdown on Sylvette's dilemma.

He didn't leave anything out, so that Vince decided to write Sylvette a letter, not to convince her to take Vincent, but to let her know what kind of a person his old school friend was, and to dispel any wrong notions about him she may have. He would send a copy to Senor Georgio, of course!

A few days later, Sylvette open her mailbox and saw this large envelope with the Royal Crest of the House of Este. In fact the mailman was just delivering, so when she opened her mailbox, the mailman asked, "Are you somebody important?"

With a slight smile on her lips she said, "Of course!"

He waited for more information but she turned to walk away when he asked, "Who are you?"

"A Princess!" She went to her apartment, and once inside giggled at what she had done. She really wasn't that far from wrong. Senor Georgio was going to see to it that she lived like one, even if it was in a minor key.

She didn't open the letter right away. She sat at the dinette table and studied the envelope, looking at the details of the family crest and trying to guess what the letter contained.

It was an amazing thing. Here was a letter all the way from far off Italy, and from Duke Antonino III Vincenti himself. She had to do some daydreaming. Did he find her a Prince to marry? Did he want her to serve as a lady-in-waiting to the Duchess Gilda?

She sniffed the envelope to see if it had some sort of Royal perfume, but it didn't. It was made of a good quality paper, though, and this would certainly be an heirloom, no matter what the letter said.

She had to open it sooner or later. She called Paula and told her about it, and Paula, acting surprised again, told the innocent girl how wonderful it was to get such a letter. Paula said, "For all the years that I have worked for the family, I never had that honor.

"Should I open it?"

Paula laughed. "Do you ever want to see what the letter says?"

"Yes, of course I do!"

"Then you'll have to open it, won't you?"

"Oh, yes! Silly me! I'll wait a while, and then I'll open it."

When Paula hung up the phone, she had to tell Senor Georgio about it. They laughed at her silliness, but it was not a mean laugh. It was a loving laugh, like one would laugh at a confused child who was nonetheless loved.

Sylvette held it up to the light, but the paper prevented her from seeing anything. She put it down and proceeded to do some unnecessary cleaning around the apartment, then went in to take a bath.

Well, she couldn't open the letter without being personally squeaky clean, could she? OK, so she dusted around, took a bath and then got comfortable. I was time to open the letter. To her dismay, she realized that she didn't have a letter opener in the apartment.

She went for a paring knife, but then decided that she couldn't open such a letter with a knife. That would be sacrilegious! So Miss Sylvette Bretey waited until morning, carried the letter to the office and asked Paula to properly open it.

Paula did all she could to hold in a loud guffaw, and in the most officious manner possible, got a fancy letter opener, and slowly inserted it under the lid and gently slit it open. She then handed it to Sylvette.

Now that it was open, she looked at it again, then carefully spread the envelope and cautiously peered inside. It the letter had come from Jesus Christ, she could not have handled it with more reverence.

With a sigh, she pulled the written pages out and began to read.

Chapter Seven

My Dear Miss Bretey,

It is my understanding that you are ambivalent about having a friendship with the junior Vincent Temperino. It is not my purpose to sway you one way or another, but I feel you should know about him so that you can see him in the natural light.

I met Vincent in Elementary School and we became friends there. He seemed to be a shy boy, but as I got to know him, I found him to be very sensible and serious, and not really shy.

We got into the habit of doing our homework together, and many times I found him to be smarter than I. He kept his homework and notebook pages so neat that I often had to read his to understand what my own work said.

I was a little better than he was in sports, but that doesn't mean he wasn't good. He was better than most and had no trouble proving it. As a team we did very well indeed.

We went through high school together; and I fully expected that we would go to college together too, so you can imagine my surprise and consternation when he said he would not attend the University. I couldn't understand. He had the grades and the ability in every way. There was nothing holding him back.

Finally he told me that he was tired of school and wanted to work with his father, and with his own hands. He loved to work with wood, and his father was in that business.

He was always a good son and got along with his parents very well. I enjoyed my years at the University, but how much better would they have been with my buddy at my side. How much fun we would have had is anybody's guess.

I studied Electrical Engineering, but Vincent didn't have to study the properties of wood, He had been helping his father for years, and knew that one day he'd take over the business.

What a lucrative business it is! He and his father are in such demand for fancy woodwork that they are never idle. This work is young Vincent's only passion, and there's nothing he can't do.

I heard about the gold-leaf cornice work in your apartment, and I'd like to see it some day. What you may like to do is visit the Temperino shop, and see not only cabinets, trimming and paneling, but also carving of statuettes and other carved forms.

Vincent and his father are both masters at woodcarving and artists in their own right. The two men are also good businessmen. No one will ever see them underestimate a project or make bad measurements and calculations.

Now, I hear you think Vincent to too shy. I have to laugh at that. Do you really think that he doesn't know his way around women? Guess again!

No, Miss Bretey, Vincent is respectful, and mindful that he had better not treat you as a lose woman, or he will incur the wrath of your benefactor, Senor Georgio.

That's right, Miss! He must keep his hands to himself, or else! Try to have some empathy for a lusty man who would love to bed you, but must be mindful of the consequences.

Vincent is not going to touch you, and you Miss, had best not seek such diversions elsewhere. That would have consequences too. You may not wish to date Vincent, That's entirely up to you, but allow me to recommend to you this course. Wait until Senor Georgio finds you a man. Believe me, you don't have much choice.

You are under the umbrella of the House of Este, and your every move must be precise. Accept your position with good grace, and you will find happiness.

Con Affetto,

Antonino Terzo Vincenti, duca d'Este

With a trembling had she gave the letter to Paula to read. When Paula looked up, Sylvette asked, "Is he mad at me?"

"Not in the least. He only wants the best for you."

"What should I do?"

"Exactly what you've been doing up to this point! He wants you to be careful, and to obey good council. Don't worry! You're doing very well. You have to expect that the family will have its eyes on you. That's the price you pay for all the care and protection. Just remember, it's well worth it, so relax and enjoy everything."

She put the letter in her purse with the intention of reading it many times and maybe even having it framed. It was a comfort to know that he cared enough to write her that way, and her mind was made up about heeding the instruction therein.

She was important to the family. That was incredible, yet it had to be true. And why? That was an enigma to her. She never though of herself as special except to her parents. Yet there was the proof. The d'Este family took her in, and valued her.

One day her phone rang, and it was Vincent. He asked her if she would like to go to a movie, but she said she's rather go to a place where they could have a nice chat.

When they met, the simple minded Vincent took her to a pizza parlor, and they sat in a booth. In his mind, this was a good place to chat. In her mind it was going to have to do. So they chatted, and she decided to tell him about the Duke's letter.

He was more than impressed. He looked at her with new eyes, realizing that she was important to the family. It was bad news to him because now it would be impossible to ask for her. At least that's what he thought.

It took a while but she began to see in him the qualities the Duke mentioned in the letter. She found herself liking him more and more, but not falling in love with him.

She was a small woman and he was a giant. Well, not a giant perhaps but big, anyway. Her womanly imagination took them to bed where surely he would crush the life out of her.

He looked at her like she was a fragile, unattainable doll. Yet, he found that he wanted her. No one else would do, but how can it happen?

They sat and chatted longer than they intended, which was the obvious sign that they had gotten comfortable with each other. What to do?

He asked his father what he should do. His father said he should go to Senor Georgio and ask for her. He disagreed! "I can't ask for her. She's some kind of a princess.

"She's a secretary's assistant, for heaven's sake. You're just awed by her and the d'Este family. Continue to date her, but mind your manners. She will give you the sign when she likes you enough."

"What sign should I look for?"

"Vincent, she's not going to paint a sign! When she looks at you with interest, and when she compliments you, or if she reaches for your hand or you arm just to touch you. Women give men certain signs. It's called 'body language'"

"She kissed me in the garden! Is that good enough?"

"It's hard to say. That may just have been curiosity on her part. Give her time. If she wants to kiss you again, then that's a sign. Also, look for certain openings. You may kiss her when the time is right."

"I'm getting it, father. I'll have to give it time."

"Well, not TOO much time!" He laughed.

"What do you mean?"

"You're not getting any younger. Give it time, but not too much time. I'm sure you'll know when it's the right time to see Senor Georgio."

Vincent shook his head, "Life is sure complicated.'"

"Only at times! Some day you'll be settled down like me and your mother, and life will be sweet."

"I'll be looking forward to it."

Chapter Eight

Sylvette took a vacation and went to see here parents. She told them about Vincent, his profession and his interest in her. Of course she got the standard advice about being careful and looking out for any bad habits he may have.

Surprisingly, he didn't seem to have any. He didn't smoke, drink or chase around at night. He was almost too good to be true. "But mama, he's such a big man, and as strong as an ox. He could crush me!"

Her mother laughed heartily. "Oh, Sylvette, you have such a vivid imagination. Why not wait until he proposes before you worry about being crushed. I can assure you that you will not be crushed. We women have a flexibility you will not believe."

"I don't understand!"

"You will! Just don't worry about it. Trust me, you will not be crushed." And she laughed again.

While she was away, Vincent was doing everything but chewing his nails. His father had to chide him for not concentrating on the job, but he also knew that the young man couldn't help himself. He was in love, and that's like a sickness. When a man falls in love he should be hospitalized until the fever is brought under control.

Vincent was marking the calendar, crossing off the days until she was to return. His parents were having a grand time seeing him so discommoded. They were hoping for this for a number of years and wondered at times if he was going to be a stay-at-home bachelor for the rest of their days.

It wasn't that they didn't like having him around, but they recognized that he deserved a complete life, with a wife and a family of his own.

Naturally, the thought of grandchildren was an anticipated attraction. What perspective grandparents don't dream of that possibility?

The slow wheels in Vincent's mind finally started turning. He realized that he was not doing anything to impress Sylvette, and the date at the pizza parlor was dull stuff. He decided to pick another place for their chats, a place that would impress even the most blasé.

After looking around and checking around, he decided on the Tavern on the Green in west Central Park. He was warned that he'd better bring a fat wallet, because it was going to be expensive.

Vincent was making good money and this was for a good cause, so he put it all together, and when his lady love returned from her vacation, he told her where he was going to take her.

At first she didn't know about the place, but Paula put her wise, and she was impressed. "Sylvette, this guy is getting serious! He just may pop the question at the Tavern."

"I'm not ready for that. I can't tell you why, but I'm not completely at ease with him. He's handsome and well mannered, but, I don't know. Maybe it's because he dresses like a carpenter."

"Oh, listen to the connoisseur of proper clothing. Shall I remind you of what you looked like when you first stepped into the office?"

"Paula, I couldn't have been that bad. I was wearing my very best."

"Ha! Your clothes shouted 'rural' loud and clear."

"Oh My! That bad huh?"

"Don't get me wrong. They fit you well enough at the time, but they would never do now. Anyway, Vincent can be dressed to look like anybody with the proper tailor, so let's not have the pot calling the kettle black!" They laughed at her parochialism, and she agreed that Vincent could be nudged into dressing better.

The night he came to pick her up he was dressed for the occasion. Her surprise was obvious as she appraised his fine suit and general appointments. "Well! Don't YOU cut a fine figure! Did somebody dress you?"

"Don't be so snippy, country girl! You forget that I was born and raised in this city. I've already forgotten what you still have to learn!"

She was momentarily take aback by his forcefulness, but then had to agree that SHE was the parvenu, and he the native. Vincent had just stepped up another rung in her opinion of him.

They had a good time. As they were chatting and laughing, they began to become aware that this place was the hangout of people watchers and the paparazzi.

One of them came closer and took some pictures of them. They couldn't explain why. They certainly could not be mistaken for being among the cognoscenti or the rich and famous

Others there were taking furtive glances at them. What was going on here? Sylvette didn't catch on that the diamond bracelet she was wearing shouted money, prestige and who knows what else."

The people watchers were watching, and both Vincent and Sylvette were getting uncomfortable with the unwarranted attention.

They decided on a walk in the park. Now there was a smart move! Walking in Central

Park wearing an expensive diamond bracelet would attract a more sordid kind of attention than they were getting at the tavern.

Sure enough, one inept robber came up holding a small switchblade knife and demanded the bracelet. Catlike, Vincent stepped in and smashed the man's nose and knocking him out completely.

"Excuse me, my dear." he said as he gently removed the bracelet from her wrist and put it in his pocket. "Perhaps I should take you home."

"No, I'm fine. Let's go and visit Marco and Cathy. Maybe they're both at Vince's apartment.

That's how they finished the night. Sylvette told them how Vincent cold-cocked the would-be robber, and Cathy, with mock appraisal, felt the muscles in Vincent's arm.

She had to be impressed. Years on the job required heavy lifting, and Vincent was up to it all. Playfully, he lifted Sylvette off the floor and spun her around like she was a rag doll.

Marco said, "Hey, hey! Muscles aren't everything! Brains count for something too."

Cathy studied her husband, but didn't comment. That brought more laughter, and the four of them started to become fast friends. This was good, because that's just what they needed as they moved among the family of aristocrats.

A few weeks later, Vincent presented himself at the Holding Company office and asked to see Senor Georgio. Paula sensed what this was all about and with some show of ceremony, shooed him in unannounced.

Standing before the desk, blushing and sweating, he stammered out that he wanted to ask for Sylvette's hand in marriage. He trembled at the thought of being refused, and wished that perhaps he should have waited for a while before jumping into the pool.

He need not have worried. Without realizing it, the plotters have been steering him toward just this very moment.

"Vincent, that is perfectly satisfactory with me! You're a fine young man from a good family Have you asked HER yet?"

"N-N-No Sir!"

"Then waste no time! Here, take this note to the restaurant indicated and you'll get a private room. After dinner, propose to her. Do you have the ring?

"No, Sir! I didn't know what you would say!"

Senor Georgio pressed a button and Paula answered. He said, "Paula, bring in the case from the safe."

She knew which case he wanted, and lost no time in getting it to him. He opened it, and looked over several rings and chose one. "What do you think, Paula? Will this one do?"

"That one is perfect! She said assuredly.

He put it back in its little box and handed it to the astounded Vincent. The dull young man still didn't get it. He sheepishly took the box, thanking them both profusely, and left for home.

Paula and the good Senor laughed and shook congratulatory hands. "Nothing succeeds like success." he fairly shouted.

Chapter Nine

Two more months had gone by after Vincent took Sylvette to the recommended restaurant, and had proposed to her, after getting Senor Georgio's kind permission.

The restaurant owner had been alerted, and the couple received the red carpet treatment, and all the other patrons present were quietly told that there was going to be a proposal, but that they should not make any fuss until the couple exited the private room.

All went well! The waiters moved quietly about as they entered the room, and the "love birds" might as well have been in church, so solemn did the evening seem.

Patrons didn't want to leave because they wanted to be in on the excitement when the two came out of their sanctuary. The result was that a line started to form in front of the restaurant with hungry diners wanting to get in.

Some of the people were grouchy, but most of them were interested in the drama that was taking place.

When they came out the crowd roared their approval, but there was a fly in the ointment. Vincent had put the ring on her finger, but SHE said she wanted to think about it.

People, seeing the ring assumed she had accepted, so they applauded and shouted all the more. Then the noise quieted down. The couple was not smiling, as they most surely should have been.

Indeed, they seemed rather sad, but no one asked any questions or anything, so they were gone before anyone made any comment. The owner didn't even get a chance to compliment them. No one understood.

Now Sylvette was really in a panic. She didn't want to hurt the feelings of her good man, but she was still on the fence about committing to him. She felt awful and so did he, but what could they do?

When the news got to the family, all they could do was wait. Any plans for the big reception and party had to be put on hold, and the family didn't like waiting when an excuse for a blowout was in the offing.

Now when the couple went around, together or singly, they were solemn and quiet, and neither one sought advice from any one, or even company for that matter. Each retreated behind his own wall, and that wall seemed impenetrable.

For everyone involved, it was just a matter of biding one's time, but it was as though a great tragedy had visited the family, in both the United States and Italy.

The conspirators had gotten together and they had hatched a general plan, but now everything was on hold. Even the Priest at Saint Jean Baptiste Church, at Lexington Avenue and 76th Street, felt some disappointment. He was already counting the money that such a wedding would bring into the coffers.

And so everybody waited. And waited! They could not prompt the pair because it could not be let out that there was this conspiracy going on. That would have spoiled the whole romantic project. Now it was the family and friends who were counting the days until the "I do's" were finally pronounced.

Certainly the impatient Vincent had done all he could! He played his role in the plan beautifully, and pretty much on key. He had to wait too, and all were sympathetic.

Sylvette felt the pressure. She knew nothing about any conspiracy, but the impatience everyone felt hung in the air and was palpable. Can anyone explain the heart of a woman? She was eager for love, and she liked Vincent, and DIDN'T WANT TO LOSE HIM.

Yet she wasn't ready to MARRY him! Figure that one out, Doctor Freud.

All right, it is true that her life since she came to New York took an almost mystical turn. Perhaps she was overwhelmed and overloaded. Could we say she was a modern day Cinderella, or something of the sort? The whole thing does read like a fairy tale, and she was just one little girl caught in a big whirlwind.

The rest of the people in the city, oblivious of the dramatic tension being played out at, and around the House of Este, went about its usual business, and everything seemed normal, at least as normal as the city ever gets.

But time heals, and one day our petite Sylvette went to Senor Georgio and said she would marry Vincent Temperino, Junior!

There wasn't a celebration in Times Square as there was when World War Two was over, but there might have been, had everyone known what was going on. There was a huge sigh of relief felt far and wide, nevertheless.

Why was there such concern by the family over the marriage or non-marriage of these two commoners? There were three reasons: First and foremost was simply the fact that the pair was loved. Secondly, the conspiracy to get them married became a game they enjoyed and wanted to succeed, and finally there was the reception, which promised to be a huge party.

They wanted a reason to have all the members of the family attending, so that they can play "catch-up with all the relatives that could make it. Could anyone think of a better reason to have a party?

The young couple didn't realize that they were now going to receive many invitations to dinner or outings, and other activities. Within the circle of family and friends, they were sort of celebrities, and people were vying to invite them.

The main result of all this was that they couldn't get very much work done. Another assistant was hired for the Holding Office, and Mister Temperino Senior hired another carpenter. No one objected to this. Once the fuss was over, everything would return to normal, and the people hired would be able to stay on anyway.

The Holding office was moving to a new building and would have more space, and the Temperino shop needed more help anyway, so it was all working out to the benefit of all concerned.

We can't say that the love birds were suffering from all this exposure. Indeed, they were reveling in it, and both of them needed to hone their social skills anyway, so it actually was an important time for them.

Francesca was not about to be left out in left field. She was in there, teaching, guiding and helping with shopping, often making the couple gifts of the things they bought. This was her thing, and she was reveling in it just as much as the kids were.

She wasn't the only one. Plans for the wedding were being laid out like a war exercise. There was in fact a place they called the "war" room and every detail for the church and the reception had to be discussed and voted on. Everyone had ideas, and these often clashed, so that sometime the "war" room became the WAR room.

Most of the time, though, they were having fun, and no one must think that they forgot the goodies that had to be brought into the room for sustenance and enjoyment.

The pizzas were arriving quite steadily, and the wine flowed like, er, wine! Tailors and dress designers came and went, and florists were consulted, not to mention jewelers and other accessory people.

The family was having a ball! For the reception, food was the main item, and that meant the hiring of extra people for the hall, despite the fact that the caterers had everything down pat. That didn't matter because the family had to put their oars into every facet of the event.

After all, that was the whole point of these parties. "Everybody wants to get into the act!" as Jimmy Durante used to say.

Even the children had to have their say. The little girls wanted to be sure of their dancing dresses, and the boys all wanted to know where the exit doors were.

Transportation was an important consideration. Certainly Sylvette's parents had to be flown in and put up somewhere. They wanted to know if the Senior Duke would come.

It was known that the Junior Duke would not come because he would be waiting for the newlyweds in Italy where they will spend their honeymoon, and preparations must be made for that.

Besides that, Duke Vince needed another party like he needed a third shoe. These sort of fusses were not his cup of tea.

Without realizing it, the family was using the best elements of logistics and strategy. Any military General would have been proud to have a crew like this group on his side.

Of course there was the usual nit-picking and posturing over who had the authority to do what, but in the main things went smoothly. There was, after all, the boss, Senor Georgio. He had the final say on everything in dispute.

Most of the time, the family could surmise what he would say, so they didn't have to call on him too often. Senora Anitra said that they were going to have a grand day. The two sweethearts were almost lost in the shuffle.

It so often happens that when people get together to organize anything, the tail starts to wag the dog. As far at Vincent and Sylvette were concerned, that was fine with them. They didn't have that much to say about the details anyway. Vincent said, "We'll just go with the flow. We don't have to know all that stuff"

Sylvette had more curiosity, but she knew he was right. Besides, they had to practice their kissing. One cannot neglect a thing like that!

Vincent said, "My darling, I think we should wait two years before we start our family so that we can better prepare for them in our own house. We should buy a house first, all right?"

"That's a sensible plan!" she said happily.

Chapter Ten.

A few days before the wedding, the police were asked to assist in traffic control. The Church was almost on the street, and the sidewalk wasn't very wide. The family needed barricades and the limousines had to be able to park.

The police were used to these occasions, so they didn't have to be advised as to what was needed. They've been through it countless times.

Still, private guards were hired to fill any gaps that the police left open. These were men who knew what the d'Este family required.

It being a Saturday, there wasn't going to be the daily traffic that filled Lexington Avenue during the week, so that would make the day easier.

The Bride and groom had their rehearsals, and were now in their proper places. The people had come in and they were in their places too.

The organist started to play, and HERE COMES THE BRIDE! The church was filled with smiles, and the groom was sweating bullets.

Mister Bretey, with his lovely daughter on his arm, came slowly down the aisle and the tears were clearly evident in his eyes.

Sylvette, her pretty face hidden by her veil, kept in step with her father, and was followed by a pretty child holding the end of her long train.

They all came together at the altar, and Mister Bretey lifted his daughter's veil, kissed her cheek and led her to the groom.

Vincent stepped in and took her hand.

While the organ played a quiet piece, the priest began in a clear voice the words that would bind these two young people together for all of their days.

The ceremony didn't take long, and soon the newlyweds were coming down the aisle and heading for the limos.

A woman on the sidewalk, seeing all the fuss, asked one of the guards, "Who's getting married?"

"A Princess of the House of Este."

"Este? Who are they?"

"The guard shrugged. If she didn't know, she could remain ignorant.

"No one threw rice. Instead they threw bird seed. When the birds ate rice and then drank water, they would get bloated and often died so this was an important consideration.

Now it was off to the reception! And now the family would shine. Everybody known well by the family was there, and some who were known by the ones who were known by the family were also there. (Did you get that?)

If someone had bothered to count they may have arrived at about two hundred or more souls, including all of the children.

The reception was staid for the first hour and a half, but then the music started and the dancing started, and the children running around like wild Indians started and it became a wonderfully Italian party.

The photographers who were busy at the church were late getting to the reception, but that was all right, because they were on time to snap Sylvette dancing the first dance with the groom and the second with her father.

It wasn't long before people had to shout at each other to be heard, which meant that this was now a typical Italian blow out. Then there was a tinkling of a little bell, and everybody quieted down while a speaker announced that the speeches were about to begin.

Of course the early speakers had to be the comedians. They told stories calculated to embarrass other people there, and those guys got back at them with stories of their own. A lot of dirt came out, and of course none of it was to be believed.

Then the more serious speeches started, and Sylvette's father had to let everyone know what a wonderful and precious daughter she was, and he was happy for both his daughter and her chosen man, and before he was finished both he and his wife were in tears

Sylvette was wiping her eyes, too. When he sat down she went over and hugged and kissed both him and her mother.

Senor Georgio's speech welcomed everyone there and also expressed his appreciation of the newlyweds. "They will have a wonderful honeymoon in Italy, and when they get back, we'll see to it that they catch up on their work!" That brought forth some laughter.

Vincent's father and mother said a few words of praise, and told a few "secrets" about their son which made everyone laugh, especially Vincent himself.

Then it was time for them to speak. Vincent got up, cleared his throat, but all he could say was how lucky he was that his precious wife agreed to marry him.

Sylvette got up and said, "You all see how small I am. Now if you look at Vincent you'll agree that I didn't marry ONE man, I married TWO men! And you know, I have no idea how much he weighs. I think I should have asked that question before I said 'yes' to his proposal."

The place roared with laughter, and Sylvette was endeared to their hearts forever. To make his own joke, Vincent picked her up and held her over his head. Some people were laughing so hard that they were knocking things off the tables.

Senor Georgio got up again and invited everyone to continue enjoying the food, and then to start dancing again.

The rest of the evening was spent dancing, eating, drinking chasing kids and generally talking to each other in loud voices.

No one noticed that the newlyweds slipped out of the hall. Marco and Cathy invited them to a small room in the back that was prepared with a bench.

Marco said, "Vincent, when Cathy and I leave the room, you drop your pants and lie down on this bench. Sylvette, you lift up your dress and sit on him. Laughing, they slipped out of the room and went back to the hall.

What happened there? Did they take the opportunity to courageously consummate the marriage? The joker Marco would make it his business to find out!

When the couple got back to the hall, they looked disheveled and flustered. "A-ha!" Marco thought. "They dooed it!" He looked over at Cathy, and she winked at him.

The great party ended late that night. By that time the lovers said their good byes and had been taken to Vince's apartment for their wedding night. Then they would be on their way to Italy the next day.

Marco went to the communication center the next morning, and found that the couple was still asleep. He roused them and told them to hurry! The plane was not going to wait for them.

The limo was waiting at the door, and the chauffeur had to do some fancy driving to get them to the plane on time.

In first class, the excited couple held hands and stole a furtive kiss occasionally, when they thought no one was watching. It may have seemed to them that no one was watching, but everyone knew what was gong on. We wonder how they knew!

The smiles on the faces of the other passengers and the flight attendants said that the couple was all too obvious in their body language. The attendants were extra solicitous, and the couple thought that this was how they treated everyone.

They didn't notice the man who was traveling in coach who came to the doorway to check on them occasionally. The flight attendants were told he was a guard hired to watch over them. One attendant asked, "Who is she?"

The guard smiled and said, "A Princess of the House of Este." The attendant knew about the d'Este family. She was an Italian-American herself.

The plane was flying into night, so the tired couple got a chance to sleep. The guard went back and closed his eyes, too.

When the plane landed in Milano, a limo was waiting for the couple on the tarmac. The couple was seated in the limo opposite the Duke, who had come to greet them. They were at a loss for words.

Vincent found his tongue and greeted Vince warmly. They began to talk about the old days, and when Sylvette was able to get a word in edgewise, she thanked the Duke for his wonderful and caring letter. "I shall treasure it always."

The limo made its usual turn into the driveway of the Castello Laura, and Sylvette was fooled, like most first-time visitors are, by the fact that the Castello could not be seen.

It was when the limo reached the crest of the hill that the top of the Castello could be seen. Then came the left turn into the drive in front of the building and the massive front doors where the staff was standing to greet the honeymooners.

They were guided through the oval foyer and into the Crystal Room where the Duchess Gilda was seated. Vincent bowed, and Sylvette curtsied and the Duchess welcomed them to the Castello.

Like magic, refreshment was served, and they enjoyed a nice chat. Others of the family came in, and the couple met Isabella, Monica, Elena and the dancer, Deli.

Then Maria Elena was brought in by her nanny, and she wanted to run to her mother, but the nanny held her tight.

In a short time, the Duchess suggested that the honeymooner be shown their room. "You must be tired from jet-lag, so rest a while and then we'll have lunch."

Duke Vince acted as interpreter, because Gilda did not speak English.

In their room Sylvette remarked at how graceful every one was, and how sweetly the talked and laughed. So this was royalty!

"Yes, and this is one of the largest occupied Royal castles left in Italy. There are larger ones, but they are either empty now, or turned into museums, occupied by schools or government offices."

"The Castle looks old on the outside."

"It is! It was built for Princess Beatrice d'Este in the 16th century."

"How nice it must be to be a Princess."

"My darling, YOU are a Princess in my eyes. I won't be able to buy you a castle or a palace, but I'll get you a house that we can make into a palace for us and our children."

"Yes, and we can do it! Vincent, I don't want to go too far in creating our dream house. We don't want to get too deep into financial debt. Let's be satisfied with something simple, but nice."

"As you said, we can do that."

They drifted off to sleep and slept right through lunch. When it got closer to dinner time, they heard a bell outside their door. Then a gentle knock and a maid came in to see to their wants.

"Maid service, Vincent! Imagine! May I have one back in the States?"

"Sure, and I'll sleep in the middle!" She punched him. The maid was puzzled by their behavior, but then, she thought Americans were all a little touched in the head anyway.

The maid helped them wash up and dress, and got then presentable for the dining room.

The family was already seated around the table, so they were shown to their seats. The Duchess said, "I don't imagine you need any more sleep," and she laughed.

Vince translated, and Vincent laughed too.

Sylvette thanked everybody and then said to Vincent, "We must learn how to speak Italian."

"I know a little of the Sicilian dialect, but that's not considered real Italian."

Duke Vince proposed a toast to the newlyweds, and everybody lifted their glasses and wished them good fortune and happiness.'

Then people began to eat and chat politely, and Vince translated some of it to the visitors. He didn't translate everything because most of it was of no interest to the couple.

Vince asked about New York city, and about his apartment and how the communications desk was being handled, and Sylvette told how she "manned" it in the absence of Marco Astuzia. Then they talked a little about the new office building and the big move to the new quarters. Vincent said that there was going to be a lot of woodwork going in because Senor Georgio liked paneling and trim.

And so the evening went until it was time to repair to the music room. Once comfortably seated there, Elena played some of her pieces on the piano, and then Elena and Vince played a few duets they had been practicing.

Vincent asked Sylvette if she would play, but she was reluctant. She whispered, "I'm not as good as they are." But The Duke knew about her playing ability, and he asked her to entertain them.

She dragged herself to the piano, thinking she was going to be a bust, but surprisingly, she settled into it and gave a good account of herself. Everyone was pleased, and they applauded and said so. Soon it was time for the family to get to bed.

The newlyweds were not at all sleepy, but they went to their bedroom and they may have found something to occupy their time. Who knows?

Sylvette learned that her mother was right. Vincent, with all his tonnage, did not squash her like a pumpkin

It seemed to them that they had just left the dinner table, and in the morning they found themselves at the breakfast table, but this time in another room.

After breakfast, the car was readied to take them to their "home away from home", the Sant'Angelo Manor. There they would be all alone to enjoy their solitude. All they would have is a cook, a maid, a chauffeur, and the Sant'Angelos themselves to show them around.

They just looked around for a few days, and then asked if they could travel. "But of course! You may do whatever you like."

"Darling, let's make the most of it. We may never come back to Italy again." So they visited Rome, Florence and Venice. By that time they were 'touristed out', so they rested and walked around the Sant'Angelo land, and went into Bergamo to dine and sight-see.

They received an invitation from Terzo to visit the Villa Laura in Neunkirchen. Vincent was eager to go because Terzo was a kindred spirit when it came to the business of wood.

They practically rushed to Austria, and Vincent and Terzo lost no time going to the forest to see the lumbermen at work, and to do some shop talking.

Regina took to Sylvette immediately, and they enjoyed the company of Regina's three boys, as she took Sylvette around the Villa for the cook's tour.

They had a wonderful and profitable day. Sylvette still had a difficult time believing that she was spending so much quality time with Aristocrats. They are so down-to-earth, she later told Vincent. He agreed.

They got back to the Sant'Angelo Manor late that night, and in the morning, Vincent wanted to see more of the land.

He went to the northern parcel and visited the structures there. He was interested in the flour mill, and was amazed at the work that was being done there. He saw that the men really worked, and that they were happy in the simple life of labor. That gave him food for thought.

He knew what hard work was, but these men didn't have to think. They were like machines, and they didn't mind that at all. Later he learned that they were the Contadini, and they were attached to the land.

The land was what they knew and respected. People came and went, even owners came and went, but the land stayed the same, and therefore they stayed the same. The land was all they needed. In the land they saw God.

He tried to talk to Sylvette about this phenomenon, but she was not capable of grasping what it is Vincent saw in them. The Contadini taught Vincent a lesson, but he was not sure what that lesson was.

He felt a strong admiration for them. They had the answers to the dilemmas of life that most men wrestle with, but never understand. It may seem strange, but something changed in Vincent, even though he wasn't aware of it at the moment.

When he saw Vince again he mention the Contadini, and Vince said, "Yes, they are wonderful, aren't they?"

So Vincent wasn't the only one who felt that. They didn't have to talk about it. This was something each man had to digest and assimilate into his own affairs, if he could figure it out.

There was only so much honeymooning and vacationing that a man can do, so one day he said to Sylvette, "It's time we got home!"

She was just about to say something, but she hesitated. It was the WAY he said it that made her pause. He was the boss, and he had spoken!

She wasn't about to argue with the gorilla. They started to pack.

Chapter Eleven

They said their good byes and thank-yous all around and soon were on the plane to New York. Home! That was where the real heart is, and that's where they belonged.

It was different on the plane going home. Where the people recognized newlyweds on the way out, they noticed nothing on the way in. It didn't take long for the "newly" in newlyweds to wear off. Now they were just "married folk", and there was nothing remotely exciting about that.

Even the flight attendants didn't seem to give them special notice. They were treated well, but not any better than the other passengers. The "aura" was gone, and that was all right with them, but if the aura was gone, what else was gone?

None of this was on their minds as the plane winged back to the Big Apple. Yet even then a certain edge had diminished. They weren't as ready to fornicate as they were before, but that wasn't the only change in Sylvette.

No, she sensed something strangely unsettling in her mind. She felt uneasy, unsatisfied, and oddly, she began thinking about satisfying her taste buds, rather than filling her vulva with pulsating male energy.

She'd rather have something tasty in her tummy, and she wanted Vincent to play with her nipples, and not anywhere else. Above all, she was having trouble thinking clearly and had the feeling that she needed more sleep that she was getting.

Vincent sensed nothing, but that comes as a surprise to no one. He had a wife now, and he loved her and cherished her, but he himself didn't think there would have to be any drastic changes in his life.

They were going to be back to work, and in two years or so, they would buy a house, and then start a family, as they had agreed on some time ago.

Someone once said that life is what happens to you while you're making other plans. Vincent had his plans, and HE was going to make his life happen.

If someone told him that the best laid plans of mice and men often go astray, it would not have registered in his head. If he could put it into words, he might have said. "I am the captain of my soul!" but he didn't have a poetic bone in his body.

He was a carpenter, and a good one! The world needed good carpenters, and he was filling his niche. That was all he had to understand. That he might have to consider the intricacies and the idiosyncrasies of women never entered his mind.

There was a surprise on the way that would knock him out of his smug complacency. Mrs. Sylvette Bretey Temperino was pregnant!

Soon, as the news came out, there will be many husbands who will smile at his shock and dismay. Husbands everywhere could tell him "Now you've got a wife, so be prepared for every surprise in the book. Sure you made plans, but what woman ever honored any plans that a man made?"

Soon they will go to a doctor, and the doctor will ask, "Are you married?"

"Yes!"

"Well?"

Yes, Vincent! Well? You unleashed your little swimmers and they swam! What did you expect?

Now what? Well, you go to work, put your shoulder to the wheel, as they say, and prepare for a little visitor. The house will have to wait. You'll have to figure out where to live, temporarily, and how to plan, temporarily!

He was in a quandary, and no one could help him. This was his red wagon, and what he didn't know was that he would be all at sea until the baby was born.

He will love the baby immediately, and all his frustrations about plans for the future will melt away, and all his plans will be for the now! He will start to dream about what the baby will be and do, and never mind that it will take years before any of those answers will be forthcoming.

One thing was predictable. When the family heard the news, they began planning a party. If the announcement of a baby on the way wasn't a good reason, what was?

A mini-war room was set up, and the plans commenced. The family even had the temerity to star picking names for the tyke. Certainly Sylvette was thinking about that, and number one on the list was Georgio, after her kind benefactor.

She was just thinking of thanking him and honoring him, but she didn't think that if it was a boy, and he was named Georgio, that child would be set for life. Sylvette was not venal, but Senor Georgio would not neglect a namesake.

And what if it was a girl? What name might be chosen her? Would Francesca be nice, after the kind and generous sister of the Duke, perhaps? She could choose little Anitra, after the kind Senora d'Este, wife of her benefactor?

The name won't matter once the baby is born, and the cry for breast milk is heard during the night, or the surprisingly odiferous diapers have to be changed.

The best laid plans! What a joke!

Chapter Twelve

The newly married's moved in with Vincent's parents until an apartment could be found. Vincent had moments when he thought, "Did I need all this? but, in the main his love for his wife was sustaining, and getting back to work was re-assuring. Remembering the Contadini, Vincent began working longer hours, and he worked as he saw them work, steadily and tirelessly.

His parents were in heaven! They catered to Sylvette's every whim, but she herself was back on the job too. She applied herself to the work and lost herself in the routine. Motherhood seemed to be a long way off.

There was plenty of work. The move to the new building was started, and people who were not used to heavier work found themselves involved in it. There were some sore muscles to contend with, but no one complained or shirked, and the move was going smoothly.

The new office was huge, and Sylvette joking told Paula that she and Vincent might make an apartment in the office. What she didn't know, and Paula didn't mention it, was the Senor Georgio was going to give them one right in the same building. The apartment was on the third floor, so Sylvette would only have to take the elevator down two stories and she was at work.

The new office and the conference room were still being fitted with paneling and trim, so the same applied to Vincent. They could both ride the elevator down and be on the job.

They would pay rent, of course, but not nearly the amount that the apartment would bring in from strangers.

Paula was about to protest, but then she remembered that Duke Piero was very generous with her years ago. Actually, she didn't feel any jealousy, and she did wish the kids a good start.

When the love birds were told that they could move into the new apartment, they were speechless! Nevertheless, it was an offer that they could not refuse.

Her belongings were moved out of her small apartment on 57th street and into the new one even before Sylvette knew it was happening. Naturally they needed more furniture and certainly a more complete bedroom, so in came Francesca to take them shopping again.

Vincent was useless, but Francesca and Sylvette knew exactly what they needed, so the buying went quickly, leaving Vincent scratching his head in amazement.

Being under the umbrella of the House of Este, and being treated like a prince, was something Vincent had to get used to. Sylvette was ahead of him on that curve, and she began to act like a princess.

The office required the hiring of new personnel. Two new girls came in, fresh out of High School, and one, Bernadette Fallon became the new assistant to Paula.

Paula's new station was in an office right outside of the main office of Senor Georgio, and she had essentially the same duties, but Bernadette Fallon had the desk in the front room near the entrance. She was the new receptionist.

The second girl, Mary Margaret Malone, became Sylvette's assistant in the file room, which was now much larger than the old file room, and gave Sylvette a proper desk. One morning she went into the room and saw a play pen! She laughed! This was surely Senor Georgio's idea, and she was going to be able to watch the baby while she worked. What a family!

One day she got up the nerve to go in and ask Senor Georgio why she wasn't promoted out of the file room, and he said, "Be patient! I have other plans for you."

She stopped at Paula's desk, but she cold not enlighten her. "He doesn't tell me everything,

Sylvette. It's possible he may make you manager of this building. That's the only opening I can see."

"I don't know how to manage a building."

"Well, I'm not sure, but I did hear a piece of a conversation the boss was having with a lawyer. There may be a separate office created for the investment and banking side of the Holding Company. I was thinking that maybe I'd get that, but he may have you in mind."

"I don't know much about that either!"

"Oh yes you do! You've been working on the accounts for some time now. Besides, he appreciates how you streamlined the system. I'll bet you're going to get that job."

"Oh, my! I'd love it if it meant a raise. We can use the money!"

"Sure you can! Come on! Vincent makes a bundle. You'll be buying a house in no time."

"Paula, I hope you're right, but the way the prices are in New York, it will be ten years before we can buy one."

"Silly! Do you think the boss will make you wait that long. He already has agents looking for a suitable place."

"Really? Oh my! I should have known! I can't wait to tell Vincent. There's no end to Senor Georgio's kindness, is there?"

"That depends, Sylvette."

One day, while Sylvette and Mary Margaret Malone were working together, Mary asked her, in all innocence, "How does it feel to be a Princess?"

Sylvette thought a while and said, "Mary, I don't know how to describe it."

Epilogue

At this writing, I cannot say whether our princess gave birth to a boy or a girl. That was not my concern in telling this story.

This story is one of luck. An innocent girl, a dreamer really, gets the idea that she could go to New York City, find a good job, make good money and maybe start a career.

Her experience in the great meat grinder that is the city could have ended quite differently, as it has for untold thousands of girls who have come in and gotten lost in the quagmire of greed, lust, insanity and cruelty.

Only the most calculating survive in New York, or those who are already positioned to make it.

To any young ladies who contemplate an honest career in the Big Apple I say, "Stay home!" The city is miss-named; it should be called the Big Shark.

The odds of you meeting a Senor Georgio are nil. Stay home, and learn to be satisfied with what you have. You can find the universe in your own back yard, if you'll take the time to look for it.

Antonino II Vincenti, duca d'Este